Books by Barbara Shook Hazen

The Gorilla Did It
Fang
Stay, Fang!

Even If I Did Something Awful

by Barbara Shook Hazen

Pictures by Nancy Kincade

Aladdin Paperbacks

Aladdin Paperbacks
An imprint of Simon & Schuster
Children's Publishing Division
1230 Avenue of the Americas
New York, NY 10020
Text copyright © 1981 by Barbara Shook Hazen
Illustrations copyright © by Nancy Kincade
First Aladdin Paperbacks edition 1992
Printed in Hong Kong
10   9   8   7

Library of Congress Cataloging-in-Publication Data
Hazen, Barbara Shook.
     Even if I did something awful / by Barbara Shook Hazen ;
Pictures by Nancy Kincade. — 1st Aladdin Books ed.
        p.   cm.
     Summary: Before revealing the awful thing she did, a child
tries to get her mother's assurance of love, no matter what.
        ISBN 0-689-71600-1
        [I. Parent and child—Fiction.   2. Love—Fiction.]
I. Kincade, Nancy, ill.   II. Title.
[PZ7.H314975Ev   1992]
[E]—dc20   91-23143

For Howard, and the original Mouser,
both really something

Mommy, do you love me?
Uh-huh.

A lot?

A bundle and a bunch.

Would you love me no matter what I did?
I sure would.

Even if I did something awful?

Like what kind of awful?

Oh, lots of kinds.

Would you still love me if I got orange crayon on the carpet?

I'd love you even if you crayoned the whole house.
But I'd make you clean it up.

Would you love me if Mouser and I were playing rough and we pulled down the dining room curtains?

I'd love you even if you played so rough you pulled
down the Empire State Building.
But I'd make you pick it up.

Would you still love me if I told a lie, like I was taking a bath, when I wasn't, when what I was really doing was sitting on the edge of the tub just swishing water?

'd love you even if you told a great big whopper and said
a whale sloshed the water all over the room. But I'd make
you mop up. And after that, you'd still have to take a bath.

Would you love me if the baby made me mad and I pinched it?

I'd love you even if you gave the baby away.
But I'd get him back.

Would you love me if I got mad at you and said
I hated you?

'd love you even if you got so mad you said you
hated me more than lima beans and sent me to the moon
with only a one-way ticket.

I would never hate you back, but I would find a way to hurry home.

But what if I did something really truly awful?
Like what?

Like playing ball in the living room after you told me
not to and breaking the vase Daddy gave you for your
birthday, even if I didn't mean to and it was an accident?
Would you still love me then?

I love you so much I'd love you if you *did* mean to and it wasn't an accident.

But I also might be mad and yell things like "I told you a thousand times!" and "This is the last straw!" and "I've had it with your disobeying!" and send you to your room with no dessert...

...and cry a little and pick up the pieces.

I'll help.

But I'd still love you no matter what, no matter how mad, no matter how awful. And I always will.

Me too, Mommy.